Trick or treat
Parakeet

Lesley Sims

Illustrated by David Semple

Parakeet can't stop to speak.
She's carving pumpkins with her beak.

It's Halloween. She can't be late.
The pumpkin judging is at eight.

She pecks too hard. One pumpkin falls...

...and lands KERSPLAT!

Look –
orange
walls!

Now Parakeet's down in the dumps.
Her perfect pumpkin lies in lumps.

She fixes it with sticky tape.

I won't win with this funny shape!

She puts the pumpkins in a row, and lights bright candles. See them glow!

The cakes and cookies soon look great
but Parakeet is running late.

"I haven't got my costume on."

Just then, the doorbell rings.
DING DONG!

She jumps in shock.
The table rocks.

She slips and knocks the sugar box.

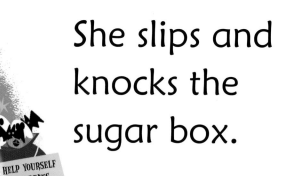

Her friends are calling from the street.
"It's trick or treat time, Parakeet!"

She flies to greet them...

"What costume?" Parakeet begins.

HELP YOURSELF
TO TREATS

Then sees her sugared face and grins.

They trick or treat on every street.
Their bags fill up with tasty treats.

But then...

...black clouds above the town.

With a KA-BOOM rain splashes down.

Poor Parakeet is sad. She groans.

"Perhaps we should head home,"
she moans.

Outside her house, they point in glee.
"Is that a ribbon we can see?"

What a Halloween surprise.
The bumpy pumpkin's won first prize!

About phonics

Phonics is a method of teaching reading which is used extensively in today's schools. At its heart is an emphasis on identifying the *sounds* of letters, or combinations of letters, that are then put together to make words. These sounds are known as phonemes.

Starting to read
Learning to read is an important milestone for any child. The process can begin well before children start to learn letters and put them together to read words. The sooner children can discover books and enjoy stories and language, the better they will be prepared for reading themselves, first with the help of an adult and then independently.

You can find out more about phonics on the Usborne Very First Reading website, **usborne.com/veryfirstreading** (US readers go to **veryfirstreading.com**). Click on the **Parents** tab at the top of the page, then scroll down and click on **About synthetic phonics**.

Phonemic awareness

An important early stage in pre-reading and early reading is developing phonemic awareness: that is, listening out for the sounds within words. Rhymes, rhyming stories and alliteration are excellent ways of encouraging phonemic awareness.

In this story, your child will soon identify the *e* sound, as in **Parakeet** and **treat**. Look out, too, for rhymes such as **box – rocks** and **fool – ghoul**.

Hearing your child read

If your child is reading a story to you, don't rush to correct mistakes, but be ready to prompt or guide if he or she is struggling. Above all, do give plenty of praise and encouragement.

Edited by Jenny Tyler
Designed by Sam Whibley

Reading consultants: Alison Kelly and Anne Washtell

First published in 2020 by Usborne Publishing Ltd., Usborne House, 83-85 Saffron Hill,
London EC1N 8RT, England. usborne.com Copyright © 2020 Usborne Publishing Ltd.